WILL HILLENBRAND

My Book Box

Harcourt, Inc.

Orlando   Austin   New York

San Diego   Toronto   London

ISBN-13: 978-0-15-202029-3   ISBN-10: 0-15-202029-2

Manufactured in Mexico

The illustrations in this book were done in egg tempera, oil pastels, and ink on canvas.
The display type was set in Worcester Round.
The text type was set in Vag Rounded.
This book was printed on totally chlorine-free Stora Enso Matte paper.
Production supervision by Pascha Gerlinger
Designed by Linda Lockowitz

To Jillian,
and all of my friends at the Public Library
of Cincinnati and Hamilton County

What can I do
with a box?

I can make a bug box....

or a pizza box...

or a pasta box....

or a hat box...

or a sock box....

or a toy box....

or a hide-and-seek box...

or a book box. Great idea!

Then I can have a book box at breakfast...

in the bathroom...

on an airplane!

travel with
my book box...

rest with
my book box....

take off with my book box.

I can even have a book-box lunch with a friend.

My book box is my treasure box.

It has everything I need.

I love to share
my book box.

But I especially
love my book box
at bedtime.

It helps me to have...

...sweet dreams.

Make your very own book box!

What you'll need:

- a cardboard box
  (one big enough to hold a stack of books)
- packing tape
- scissors
- construction paper
- stickers
- glue
- crayons, colored pencils, or markers
- a pile of your favorite books

1 Have a grown-up help you cut the flaps off the top of the box and reinforce the bottom of the box with packing tape.

2 Decorate the outside of your box with pictures, cutout shapes, or stickers.

3 Fill your box with your favorite books.

It's that easy. You're done!

Last, but not least, enjoy your book box!